WHERE'S ELEPHANT?

Moira Gardener illustrated by – Debra Datzkiw

WHERE'S ELEPHANT?

For all of those who have or have had a special childhood friend. – MG

Published in Canada by Moira Gardener
For more information:
www.moiragardener.com

ISBN Soft Cover 978-0-9868114-0-1
eBook ISBN 978-0-9868114-1-8

Printed and bound in Canada by Island Blueprint
Typeset & Cover Design: Greg Salisbury of Red Tuque Books

... fun at the
pet shop with
Santa

... Cocoa at
Cher's Cafe

... then disaster struck

He got
left behind.

"ELEPHANT!"

They looked under the seats

... On the floor

... in the car
toy bag.

NO
ELEPHANT!

"It's OK, he must be at one of the shops," said Daddy. "I'll be back."

Leaving mom and Sam at home Daddy drove ...

... to Cher's Cafe. Where he looked under the tables ...

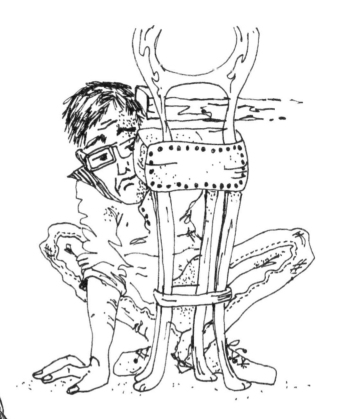

... rummaged through the lost and found box.

NO ELEPHANT!

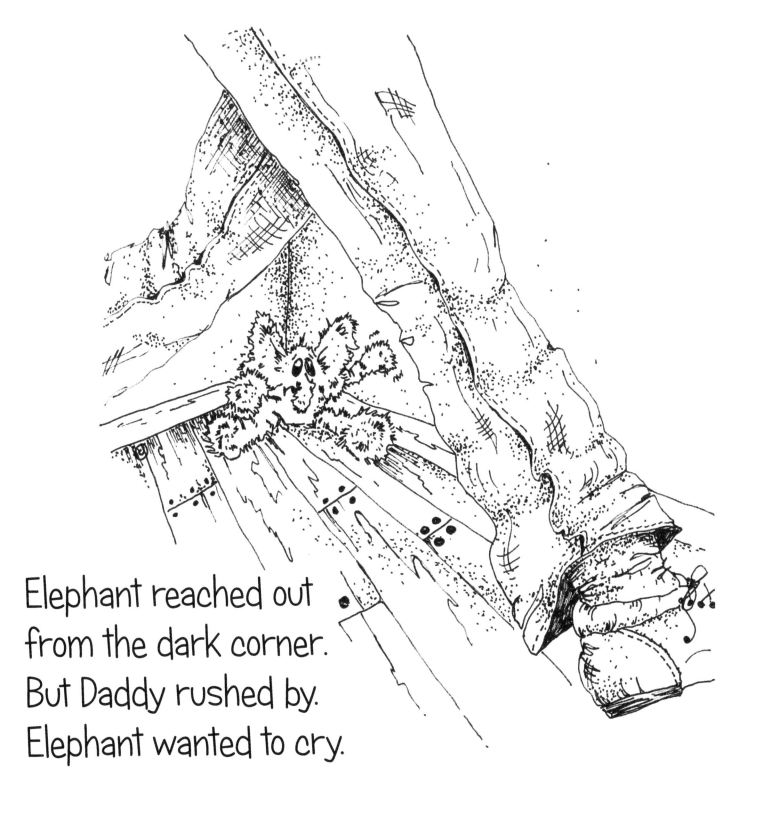

Elephant reached out
from the dark corner.
But Daddy rushed by.
Elephant wanted to cry.

Daddy went back to the pet store. "Have you seen Elephant?"

The elf looked ...

... and looked

... and looked

NO ELEPHANT!

Daddy grew worried as he watched a poodle leave the pet shop with a toy.

Daddy pulled into the driveway.

"Sorry little buddy. No Elephant!

... but I have
an idea."

Being a man of action Daddy opened his computer. Together Sam and Daddy made a poster to put online and around town.

The town folk rallied around to search for Elephant.

Marisa Coleman saw the poster and phoned. "I have an elephant; would you like to have him?"

Sam shook his head, "No thank you."

The sitter stopped by. "Hey Sam, here is the elephant I had when I was a kid. Would you like to have him?" Sam looked it over, "No thank-you."

At the supermarket Mrs. Mackey hobbled over.
"Find elephant Sam?"
"No, Mrs. M."
"H-m-m, don't give up."

Elephant had been missing for a whole week.

While Sam slept ...

Daddy looked at *every* online toy store and ordered another elephant.

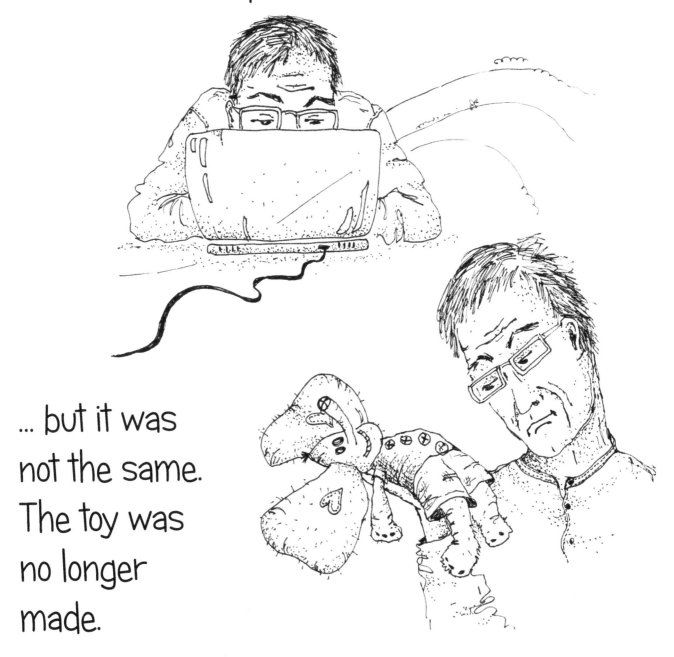

... but it was not the same. The toy was no longer made.

Sam took the new elephant to bed. But
it was not the same. Sam and Elephant
had shared so many adventures, the
new elephant was a stranger.

"This one," she pulled Elephant out of the lost and found. "I think I found your owner." Elephant's ears perked up at the word '*owner*.' Then she snapped a photo.

"Cher, keep this guy
in the back. He's
real important."

"I swear he's
smiling."

At the bookshop she opened her computer. She keyed in, *Elephant at Cher's Café*, then added the photo.

"Hurrah!" Daddy cheered.

He rushed to Cher's Café just
as Cher was locking up.

Cher grinned
as she got
Elephant.

The look on Daddy's face as she handed him Elephant made her day.

Sam had stopped asking about elephant and was playing with his cars.
"Guess who I found Sam."

Sam looked up as Daddy brought elephant out. Sam's face lit up. Daddy's heart filled up.

"Elephant will never get lost again. We will make him a special tag."

Sam and Elephant liked that. A LOT.

9 780986 811401